Penelope Harper
Illustrated by Cate James

Lollipop's family are at the seaside.

Dad is trying to put up the deckchair.

Mum is reading her book.

Little brother James is playing in a BIG hole.

And Grandpa is getting
himself into a bit of a pickle.

"It's a risky business being here, on the Jurassic Coast."

Lollipop is a bit puzzled.
"Why is it called the Jurassic Coast, Grandpa?"

"Because we're in dinosaur territory!" says Grandpa, his eyes wild with excitement.

"But the dinosaurs died out millions of years ago," says Lollipop.

"Nonsense!" cries Grandpa. "Dinosaurs aren't extinct.

They're just very good at hiding!"

"Would you like to go on a dinosaur hunt, Lollipop?" asks Grandpa, limbering up, ready for action.
"We can follow my secret dinosaur trail."

"Yippee!" shouts Lollipop, and they set off across the sand.

They haven't gone very far when Grandpa drops to his
knobbly knees, and plucks something from the shingle.
"What is it?" asks Lollipop.

"It's a fossil," explains Grandpa.
"It's our proof that the dinosaurs are still here . . . if we can find them."

At the cliff face there are lots of men
at work, shovelling and hammering.

"Lollipop, we've got a whopper already!"
whispers Grandpa.

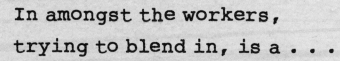

In amongst the workers,
trying to blend in, is a . . .

...DIGGERO-DOCUS!

"WOW!" exclaims Lollipop, flicking through her Dinosaur Guidebook.

"That's definitely one for the album," says Grandpa.

CLICK!

"Say LEAVES!"
says Lollipop.
"That's what a Diggero-Docus
likes to eat."

"The trail points UP!" says Grandpa, and they climb the steep steps of the cliff.

They're out of puff and nearly at the
top, so they stop to admire the view.

"Grandpa, Grandpa! I can see one!"

Lollipop takes out her Dinosaur Guidebook
and sure enough, they've just climbed up
the back of a . . .

"**WOW!** Now that is a brilliant hiding place!" exclaims Lollipop, as Grandpa does a celebratory jig.

It's REALLY blustery on top of the cliff,
and Lollipop and Grandpa have to hold on tight
to one another.

"To the trees, Lollipop!
And don't forget to hold on to your haaaaaaaaaaaat!"

'"Phew," says Lollipop, as
they make it out of the wind.

It's dark in the trees,
and there are lots of
strange noises.

Suddenly, Grandpa stops in his
tracks.
    It's a . . .

...TRY-SEE-THE-TOPS!

"He's incredible!"gulps Lollipop.
"We're getting some good ones today," grins Grandpa.

Grandpa LOVES dinosaur-hunting, and Lollipop has
to admit...he's pretty good at it!

It's a bit cold in the woods, so Lollipop and Grandpa head out into the sunshine. But a dark shadow falls across them.

"Oh my!" gasps Grandpa, under his breath.

Lollipop slowly lifts her head, to take in the enormous shape that's looming over them.

Hardly daring to move, Lollipop opens the Dinosaur Guidebook.

"Grandpa, it's a . . . it's a . . .

...PYLON-A-SAURUS REX!"

"Lollipop," whispers Grandpa,
"I think it's our turn to hide.

Run for it, Lollipop!"

But Lollipop has a better idea.
Quick as lightning, she grabs
the camera and, this time,
the Pylon-a-Saurus Rex is dazzled and
dazed. And by the time he opens his
eyes . . .

Lollipop has vanished.

FLASH!

"I thought WE were going
to be lunch for a moment
there!" says Grandpa.

"But this is a top-notch
place to hide."

When they finally get back to the beach,
there's no sign of the Pylon-a-Saurus Rex.

Lollipop and Grandpa show their photographs to
Mum, Dad and little brother James.

"Lollipop!
That one's right up my nose!" cries Grandpa.

"But they were here!"
cries Lollipop, who is getting very annoyed.
"We did see them."

"Don't worry, Lollipop," says Grandpa.
"Dinosaurs are very good at hiding.
　　　　　But just remember..."

... they're not as good as we are."

Lollipop and Grandpa's Dinosaur Guide

The Jurassic Coast, in Dorset, has cliffs that are around 180 million years old.
The coastline is named after the Jurassic Period, when dinosaurs roamed the earth.

Diggero-Docus/Diplodocus
(Di-plod-oh-kuss)

Diplodocus was a plant-eating dinosaur.
He had a VERY long neck and a VERY long tail to balance him out.
He would whip his tail around at any predators that tried to attack him.

Stair-go-saurus/Stegosaurus
(Steg-oh-sore-us)

The Stegosaurus had bony plates all along its
back and a spiky tail, which it used to defend itself.
He was a plant-eater, but not a very bright one.
Despite his size, the brain of a stegosaurus
was the size of a walnut.

Try-see-the-tops/Triceratops
(Try-serra-tops)

Triceratops had three horns on his face and a
big beak, like a parrot. He had a large frill
around his head, which could be up to one metre
across. Despite his horns and beak, Triceratops
was also a plant-eater.

Pylon-a-Saurus Rex/Tyrannosaurus Rex
(Tie-ran-oh-sore-us rex)

Tyrannosaurus was a fearsome meat-eater, with powerful jaws and
around sixty terrifying teeth. He could crunch through bones, and
used his keen sense of smell to hunt his prey.
He grew up to twelve metres long and was the king of the dinosaurs.